From the author
and illustrator of
*Mr. Mehan's Mildly Amusing
Mythical Mammals*

The Handsome Little Cygnet

written by

Matthew Mehan

illustrated by

John Folley

Illustrated by John Folley
Graphic design by Caroline Green, Matthew Mehan, and John Folley

Library of Congress Control Number: 2021937764

ISBN: 978-1-5051-2060-8

Published in the United States by
TAN Books
PO Box 269
Gastonia, NC 28053
www.TANBooks.com
Printed in the United States of America

In loving thanks for our fathers, our mothers,
our wives, our children,
and our friendship.
—Matthew Mehan & John Folley

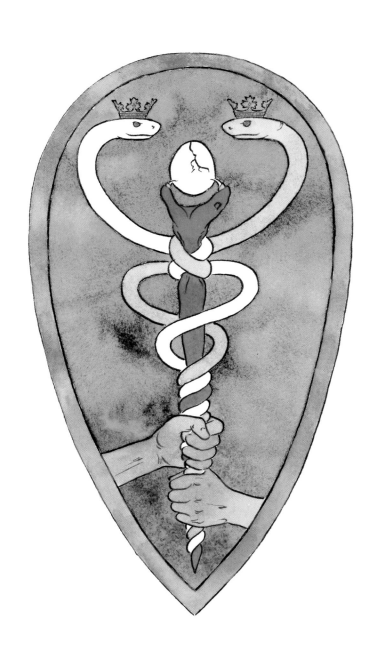

Cygnet – [sĭg·nĭt] a young swan

—from Noah Webster's American English Dictionary (1828)

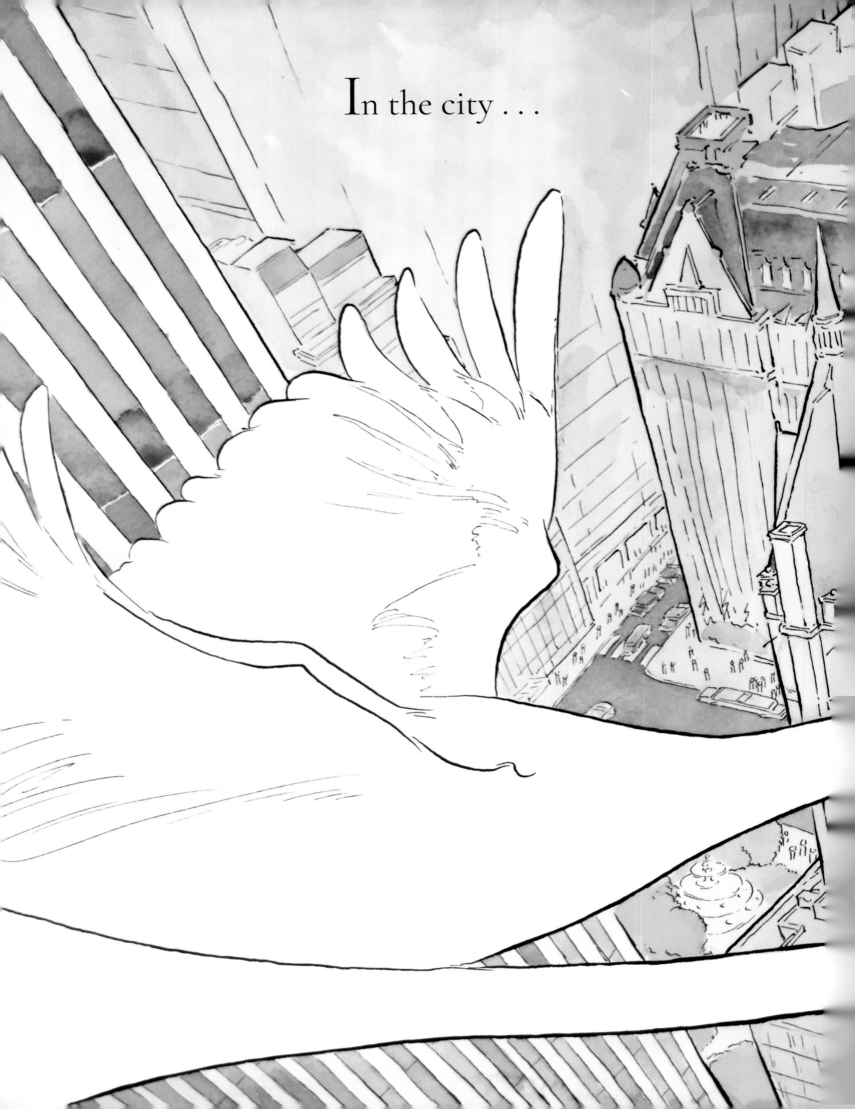

In the city . . .

On a handful of
man-made lakes . . .

A family of swans began one spring
to raise a handsome little cygnet.

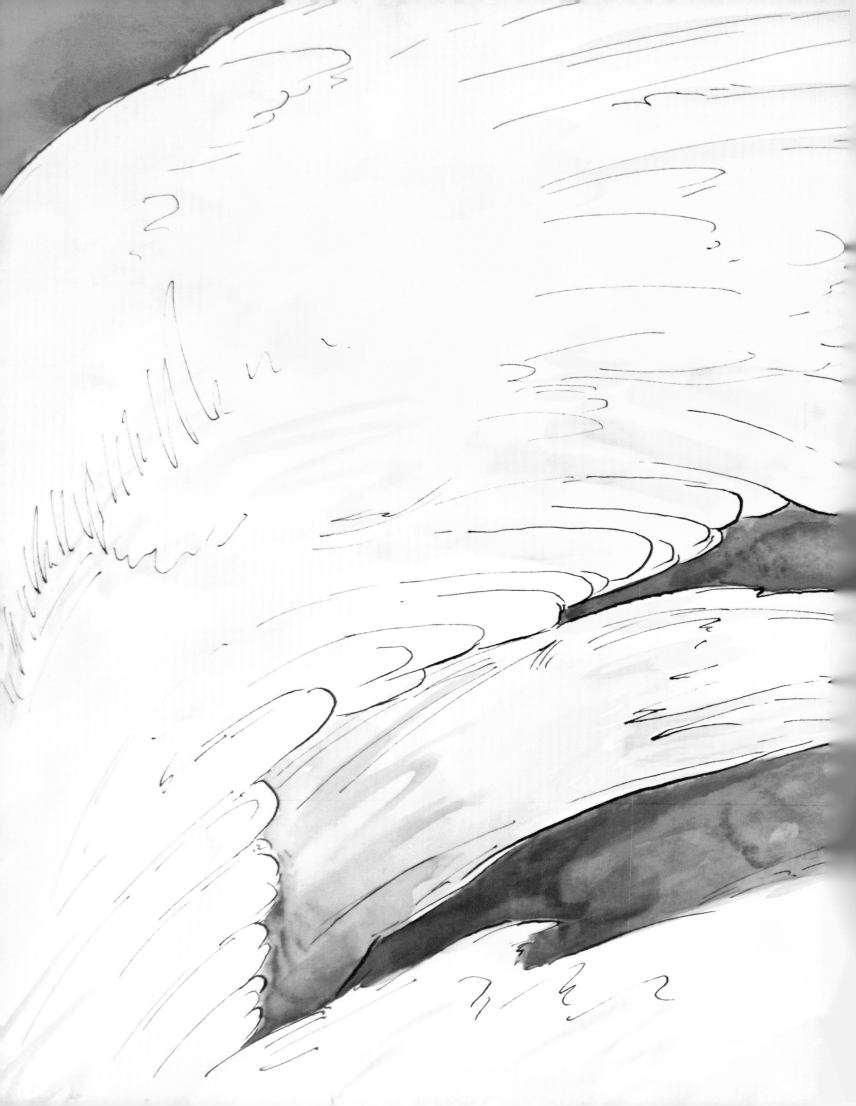

Mother and father
swans bond for life,
and these two loved their
little cygnet very much.

As summer arrived,
Father Swan would say,
"Handsome little cygnet, so dear
to me, stay close to your mother,
and stay close to me."

And the handsome little cygnet
would quickly reply, "I will, I will!
I love you so. Why would I wander?
Where would I go?"

And Father Swan would sometimes reply, "Good. Good. But little cygnet, you must know, a swan's heart can wander where a swan can never go."

And while his heart did not wander,
the handsome little cygnet waddled far
and wide, in the full bloom of summer,
with his mother and father.

Until one day . . .

So the handsome little cygnet rolled and rolled, and the colors stained every feather and fold. His soft handsome down went from gray to greenish-brown. And his feathers clumped, and some stuck to the ground.

The handsome little cygnet, with a tear in his eye, paddled to his mother and gave out a cry, "O Mother! Mother! What shall I do? I rolled in the colors that a vandal just drew. I thought I should try to be something I'm not, and now look at the ugly brown stains I have got!"

"'What to do?' you ask? O my handsome little cygnet," Mother Swan replied, "I'm not sure I know. But perhaps ask the fish who reside in the water below."

SPLOOSH!

The handsome little cygnet was so surprised, he looked at the fishes with widening eyes.

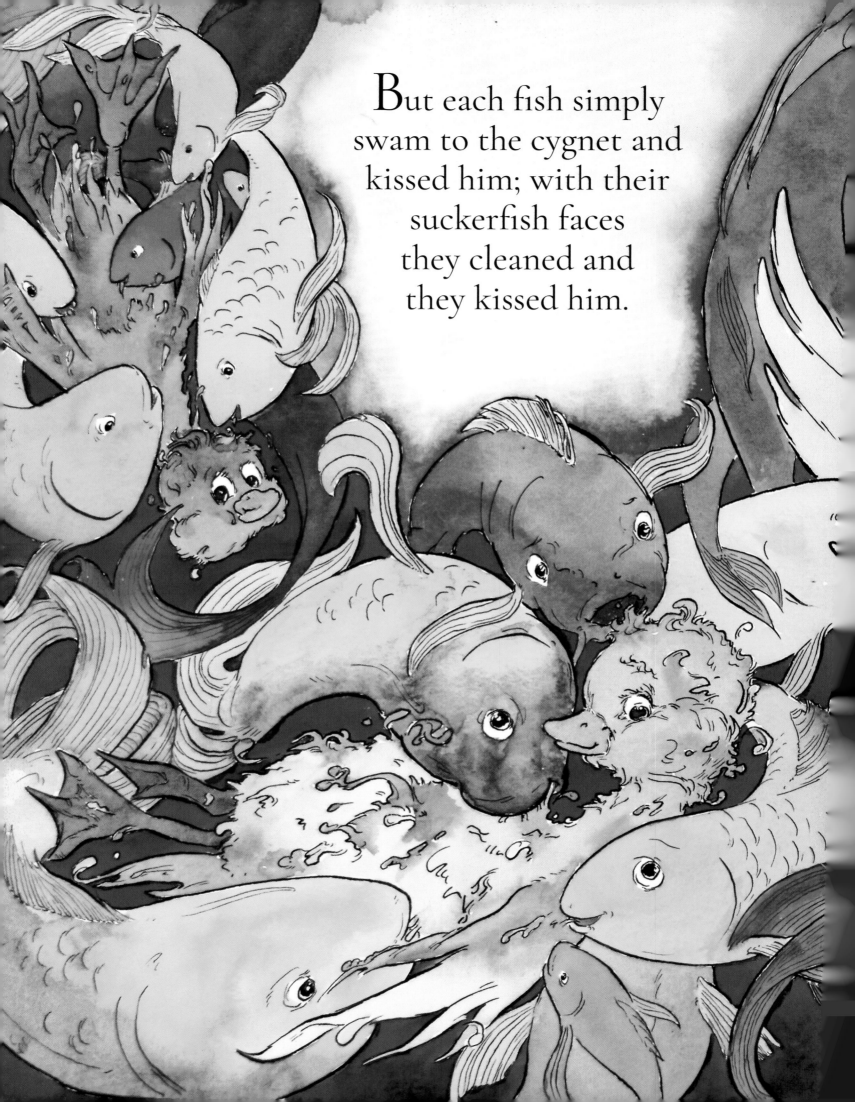

But each fish simply swam to the cygnet and kissed him; with their suckerfish faces they cleaned and they kissed him.

Just as soon as it happened, just that soon did it end, when his mother pulled him up from the water again.

The handsome
cygnet was gray once
more, and his father spoke
as he'd spoken before:
"Handsome little cygnet, so
dear to me, stay close to your
mother, stay close to me."

And the handsome cygnet carefully replied, "I will. I will. I love you so. I've no wish to wander when I finally must go."

And Father Swan answered with
gentle love: "O my handsome cygnet,
we know that you must leave us,
when you have grown. Yet even then,
we three swans will not be alone."

The End